Where Does Pepper Come From?

And Other Fun Facts

Where Does Pepper Come From?

By Brigitte Raab

Illustrated by Manuela Olten

Black pepper comes from the berries of the pepper plant. The berries are picked while still green and then dried. Black pepper is the most common spice in the world, and it adds a hot, spicy taste to food. Most pepper is grown in India, Indonesia, Brazil, and Malaysia.

Translated by
J. Alison James

Why do bears
hibernate in winter?

Because they can't find winter coats big enough to fit them!

No!

In the winter there is not enough food for bears to eat. That is why they eat enough food in the fall to last them through the winter. Then they spend the coldest time of the year sleeping in caves.

Because they love to go camping!

8 inches

No!

The shell of a snail protects it from predators and from the hot sun.

Because a sea captain
sprinkled salt on the water.

The salt is in the rocks and stones of the earth. Rain soaks through the ground, dissolving salt along the way. The salty water runs into streams and rivers, which carry the salt to the oceans.

Sea Salt

Sea

Because they're embarrassed about being stared at in the zoo.

No!

Flamingos eat a lot of small shrimp, crabs, and algae, which have the same red carotenoid pigment that carrots have. That's why they turn pink.

Because they love to put it up in curlers!

Sheep's wool is naturally curly. The curls create pockets of air that keep the sheep warm in cold and windy weather.

Why isn't a whale a fish?

Because whales are too big
to fit into any aquariums.

Most fish lay eggs, but whales give birth to live babies. Whales are mammals, and whale babies drink milk from their mothers.

Why don't migrating birds get lost when they fly south in the fall?

Because they have
compasses in their beaks!

Migrating birds actually do have a kind of compass in their beaks that helps them to find their way. Birds also orient themselves by the sun and the stars.

Text and illustrations copyright © 2005 by Verlag Friedrich Oetinger, GmbH, Hamburg, Germany

English translation copyright © 2006 by North-South Books Inc., New York

First published in Germany by Verlag Friedrich Oetinger
under the title Wo wächst der Pfeffer?

Published in the United States, Great Britain, Canada, Australia, and New Zealand in 2006
by North-South Books, an imprint of NordSüd Verlag AG, Gossau Zürich, Switzerland.

Distributed in the United States by North-South Books Inc., New York.
Library of Congress Cataloging-in-Publication Data is available.
A CIP catalogue record for this book is available from The British Library.

ISBN-13: 978-0-7358-2070-8
ISBN-10: 0-7358-2070-8
1 3 5 7 6 9 10 8 6 4 2
Printed in Belgium